W9-AOF-182

RENEE BEAUREGARD LUTE

Winicker
Wallace

FONDUES RACLETTES

L'AUBERGE

Winicker Hates Paris

ILLUSTRATED BY LAURA HORTON

Calico

An Imprint of Magic Wagon
abdopublishing.com

For Maddie, Simon, and Cecily, who inspire me, for Zach, who encourages me, and for my mom, who's told even her hair stylist about Winicker. —RL

To Mom, who inspired me to be curious about new places and cultures. —LH

abdopublishing.com

Printed in the United States of America, North Mankato, Minnesota.
102017
012018

THIS BOOK CONTAINS RECYCLED MATERIALS

Written by Renee Beauregard Lute
Illustrated by Laura Horton
Edited by Heidi M.D. Elston
Art Directed by Laura Mitchell

Publisher's Cataloging-in-Publication Data

Names: Lute, Renee Beauregard, author. | Horton, Laura, illustrator.
Title: Winicker hates Paris / by Renee Beauregard Lute; illustrated by Laura Horton.
Description: Minneapolis, Minnesota : Magic Wagon, 2018. | Series: Winicker Wallace
Summary: Winicker Wallace is forced to move to Paris when her mother starts a new job. She cannot find a single thing about Paris that she likes, except maybe that her Grandma Balthazar is there with her. It rains too much. Winicker's neighbor is irritatingly perfect. And, there is a mean girl in class who makes Winicker want to jet right back to her old house in Massachusetts. When Winicker finds herself in a scary situation, she must accept help from an unexpected source and may finally see a silver lining behind all of those Parisian rain clouds.
Identifiers: LCCN 2017946579 | ISBN 9781532130519 (lib.bdg.) | ISBN 9781532131110 (ebook) | ISBN 9781532131417 (Read-to-me ebook)
Subjects: LCSH: Parent and child--Fiction--Juvenile fiction. | Employees--Relocation--Juvenile fiction. | France--Paris--Juvenile fiction. | Humorous Stories--Juvenile fiction.
Classification: DDC [FIC]--dc23
LC record available at https://lccn.loc.gov/2017946579

Things I Hate about Paris:

1.) EVERYTHING IS DIFFERENT IN PARIS 6

2.) MIRABEL PLOUFFE IS THE WORST 16

3.) WE ONLY HAVE ONE BATHROOM 27

4.) MY NEW SCHOOL IS TERRIBLE 38

5.) EVERYBODY IS ALWAYS MAD AT ME 50

6.) PAY TOILETS ARE VERY DANGEROUS 64

7.) MAIZY DURAND IS THE WORST 73

8.) EVERYTHING IS OLD AND CRUMBLY 81

9.) IT IS TOO EASY TO GET LOST 90

10.) PARIS ISN'T WHAT I EXPECTED 99

Dear Reader,

I don't know your actual real name, so just pretend your name is in the place where I wrote "Reader."

There are some French words in this book, because this book takes place in Paris. When you see a French word that you don't know, just flip to the back of the book! There is a glossary back there that will tell you what *bonjour* and *merci* mean, and lots of other French words, too.

I know what you are thinking. "Wow, thank you so much! That is really helpful."

You're welcome. I hope you enjoy this very amazing and hilarious story.

Love,

Winicker

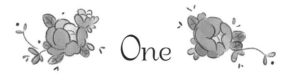

One

I hate Paris. My parents say, "Winicker Wallace, you do not hate Paris." But I do. I am eight, and that is old enough to know what I hate. Before we moved to Paris, I wore my hair in two buns on top of my head. Now I wear one single, sad bun.

Grandma Balthazar calls it a protest. A protest is when you want to show your parents how much you hate Paris. But they asked you to stop saying I hate Paris, especially in public. So you wear your hair in a single sad bun to remind them without getting yelled at.

I am sad because we live in Paris now. I am sad because we do not live in my favorite town, which is Three Rivers. I am sad because we do not live in my favorite state, which is Massachusetts. I am sad because we do not even live in my favorite country, which is the United States of America. And I am sad because we live thousands of miles away from my best friend, Roxanne.

Two weeks ago, my mother started her new job in Paris. Paris is not in Three Rivers or Massachusetts or the United States of America. Paris is in France, and I do not speak French.

This morning, my family is smooshed around a tiny table inside a café with a long name. There are ugly paintings of fruit and dead flowers all over the walls. There are bookshelves that go all the way up to the ceiling. There are a million dusty books.

"Ah. Ah! ACHOO!" I wipe my nose with the back of my hand. "I'm allergic to Paris," I say to my mom and dad and Grandma Balthazar. This is different than saying I hate Paris. This is a health problem.

·· 7 ··

Grandma Balthazar pours coffee into her cup. "You'll learn to love Paris. You just need to give it a chance." Grandma Balthazar dresses fancier in Paris. Back home in Three Rivers, she wore a pink sweatshirt that had a puffy white cat on the front.

In Paris, Grandma Balthazar wears loose shirts and leggings. She wears scarves and puts sunglasses on her head like a headband. She says "When in Rome." But we aren't in Rome. We're in Paris. Everything is already different. I don't understand why her clothes need to be different, too.

I push away my plate of waffles. They smell good, but I am protesting. "I did give it a chance," I say. "It's cold and rainy, and I miss my friends. Especially Roxanne, who makes the best fluffernutter sandwich in the world."

I squeeze the heart-shaped Best Friends necklace I am wearing. Roxanne gave it to me before I moved to Paris. Actually, it is my 'Be Fri' necklace. Roxanne has the other half, and her half says 'st ends'. When I squeeze it, I feel a little like Roxanne isn't thousands of miles away. I feel a little like she could be right down the street, eating pancakes with Granny Bee.

Granny Bee is Roxanne's grandmother. Granny Bee is short for Granny Becky, which is short for Granny Rebecca.

My stomach makes a loud gurgling sound. My waffles are buttery and steaming. I wish I hadn't pushed them away.

Dad leans his elbows on the table. "Let's break this down," he says. "It is cold and rainy here, sometimes. But it's sometimes cold and rainy in Massachusetts, too."

Mom smiles at me. "And you'll make lots of friends when school starts tomorrow."

Grandma Balthazar nods her head. "Maybe one of them will make great sandwiches, too." She takes a sip of her coffee and brushes a hand over her pile of silver hair. I love Grandma Balthazar's hair. It's gotten even more silvery since we moved to Paris. I miss her cat sweatshirt, but I like her new hair.

"Yeah, maybe," I say. But I don't think I will make lots of friends tomorrow. And I really don't think any of them will ever make a fluffernutter sandwich as well as Roxanne.

I keep my head down on the rainy walk to the Métro. I squeeze my necklace the whole way. I keep my head down when we step into the Métro station, too. But then we have to squash past a whole bunch of people who are getting on or off the train.

I look up while we walk through the station. I'm afraid I am going to get separated from Mom and Dad and Grandma Balthazar in the crowd. There are too many people. It's hard not to get bumped away from my family.

If only Grandma Balthazar still wore her pink sweatshirt with the cat on the front. Then it wouldn't be so hard to keep track of her in a crowd. But now she dresses like all of the other people in Paris. So it is actually very hard to keep track of her in a crowd.

But I don't get separated. A lady with a giant red purse bumps into me. I trip. Then I go crashing into a man wearing a real baby on his chest. The baby is in some kind of backward baby backpack.

"Sorry!" I say, but the man doesn't smile at me. Maybe he doesn't speak English. I don't know how to say sorry in French.

We finally get through and step onto the train. I am crammed in the middle of Mom and Dad and Grandma Balthazar. And Mom and Dad and Grandma Balthazar are crammed in the middle of a thousand French strangers. I feel like a crayon in a too-full box.

Crayons remind me of school. And school makes my stomach feel like a balloon full of bees. I reach for my 'Be Fri' necklace. It isn't there! I shake my raincoat to see if my necklace falls out the bottom. It doesn't.

"Mom! My necklace is gone!" I push against Mom and Dad and Grandma Balthazar. I bend down to look for my necklace on the floor. I can't see anything! Just French peoples' shoes and boots. I stand up again. "It's gone!"

"What necklace?" Dad looks concerned.

"My 'Be Fri' necklace from Roxanne!"

"Be Fri?" Dad says. He scratches his chin.

Our train slows down and then stops. Lots
of the people around us get off when the doors
open. Now I have lots of room to kneel down and
search the floor.

"Oh honey, the floor is probably filthy!" Mom is grossed out. And she's right. The floor is really filthy. There are little crinkled up receipts and gum wrappers. There are all different colors of crumbs—yellow and white and pink and green. I wonder whether the green crumbs started out green, or if they turned green after being on the floor of the train for a while.

There is a broken hair elastic and a comb. Maybe they belonged to the same person. There is half of a blue button, too. But there is no 'Be Fri' necklace.

"What in the world is a 'Be Fri' necklace?" Dad asks.

"Honey, let's go home. This is our stop. You probably left your necklace in your room this morning. It'll turn up!" Mom gives me a smile.

"No! I had it at the café, and I had it when we walked to the Métro. And now it's gone! And I'm never going to find it!"

We all step off the train and into the station. There is a bench against one of the Métro walls. I sit down on it.

My face feels all crumpled up like an old paper towel. A big tear rolls down my cheek. I don't care that strangers are looking at me. I cry and cry and cry. Mom and Dad rub my shoulders, and Grandma Balthazar makes a *shhhhh* noise. But I don't stop crying. I hate Paris.

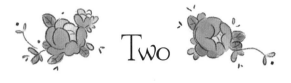

Two

We get home to our new apartment. Which isn't new at all. It's about a million years old. I sit down hard at our kitchen table. My face feels tight from crying so much. I keep reaching up to touch my necklace, but there is nothing there. Just my neck.

Mom snips the stems off flowers she bought. They smell like soap. Dad clangs and bangs through the cabinets for a vase. Grandma Balthazar sits down next to me. She smells like soapy flowers too. She used to smell like peanut butter cookies.

Outside the kitchen window, all I see is the rain and the courtyard and the road. And then I see the rain and a passing car. And then I see the rain and a passing car and awful Mirabel Plouffe walking in the courtyard.

Mirabel Plouffe is eight years old, too. She lives in the apartment next to us. At night, I can hear Mirabel Plouffe practicing her awful clarinet. In the afternoon, I can hear Mirabel Plouffe watching the French news. No ten-year-olds watch the news in Three Rivers. In the morning, I can't hear Mirabel Plouffe at all. But I bet she's doing something awful. Like having a teddy bear tea party in her super-clean bedroom.

"I just thought of another thing," I say. Everyone looks at me. "Mirabel Plouffe! She's the worst."

Mom frowns. "Mirabel is a very nice girl. She and her parents have been very welcoming!"

I look at Mirabel Plouffe again. She's walking in the rain with a fancy red umbrella and shiny red boots. And a shiny silver necklace that I can't see very well through the window and the rain.

But I bet it doesn't say 'Be Fri' or 'st ends' or anything. I bet it has a poodle on it.

She sees us all looking at her, and she smiles and waves. I push the end of my nose up with my finger so it looks like I have a pig nose. Mirabel Plouffe stops smiling.

"Winicker Wallace!" Mom says in her mad voice. "I know you're having a bad day. But that doesn't mean you get to be rude to our neighbor!"

"I'm not having a bad day," I say. "I'm having a bad month! I'm having a bad year! I'm having a bad life!"

"Okay," Mom says. "I think you need to go to your room and take a break."

When Mom tells me to take a break she means go have a time-out.

I go to my room and flop on top of my puffy blue comforter. My eyeballs feel hot and watery. I blink until tears squeeze out.

I miss Three Rivers. I miss Roxanne. I miss my 'Be Fri' necklace, which probably fell into the sewer. Or maybe it got kicked onto the tracks and smashed into a million pieces by the train. Or maybe a crow flew away with it. Or maybe another kid found it and is wearing it right now, even though she's never even met my best friend, Roxanne.

That last thought makes me feel sadder than all of the other ones.

Grandma Balthazar opens my door a crack. "Can I come in, or is this Winicker time?"

I pat my comforter. Grandma Balthazar comes in and sits down next to me.

"Okay, Winicker. I understand that you don't like the rain or Mirabel Plouffe. I understand that you're feeling very, very sad about losing your necklace. And I understand that you miss your friends. Especially Roxanne. But let's try to think of all the friends you'll make here."

"I won't if all the girls here are like Mirabel Plouffe. She's awful." I roll over and bury my face in my pillow.

"No," says Grandma Balthazar, "not awful. A bit of a goody-goody, but not awful. And there will be all sorts of girls at your new school! Weren't there all sorts of girls at your old school? It will be like that." Grandma Balthazar runs a hand through her silvery hair. The blue and gray stones in her rings sparkle.

"I wish you didn't dress fancier than you used to," I mumble into my pillow. I miss her cat sweatshirt.

"Well, I wish you didn't wear your hair in a single bun. It reminds me that you're feeling sad, and that makes me sad."

I roll over and wipe my eyes. "Your hair is different, too. More silvery. It's different than it was in Three Rivers. But I like it."

Grandma Balthazar touches her hair and laughs. "So do I. See? Sometimes change is a good thing! I guess that's the magic of bottled hair color. But I miss the old Winicker's two buns. Are they going to make an appearance anytime soon?"

"Maybe," I say, but I doubt it. I'll probably feel sad for a long time. Maybe forever.

Grandma Balthazar leans in and gives me a big hug. I almost don't notice that she smells like soapy flowers.

"Okay. Good. And here's the thing. Mirabel is waiting in the kitchen with your mom and dad. Her parents sent her over to say hello to you. I bet it would make your parents really happy if you'd just say a quick hello and try to be nice. No more pig noses. Do you think you can do that?"

I do not like Mirabel Plouffe. But Grandma Balthazar looks really hopeful, so I say "okay." She gives me another hug and then dances out into the kitchen. Grandma Balthazar even walks fancier in Paris. Like she's in a ballet or something.

Mirabel Plouffe's cheerful face appears in my doorway. "Winicker! Bonjour!" She pokes her head into my room and looks around. Her necklace doesn't have a poodle on it. It has a tiny silver chicken.

She wrinkles her nose at the model of the USS *Constitution* hanging above my bed. That is a very famous ship from Massachusetts. She frowns at my poster of Boston. That is a very famous city in Massachusetts.

"I am here to say hello!" Mirabel Plouffe must have taken her shiny red boots off in the kitchen. She's wiggling her toes in socks that have little black polka dots all over them.

"Hello, Mirabel Plouffe," I say. I say Mirabel Plouffe's whole name because it is the closest thing to a bad word I can say without getting in trouble.

Mirabel Plouffe smiles a big, white smile. "Are you ready for school to start tomorrow?" She has a French accent, but her English is perfect. She is probably perfect at every language.

"I guess," I say.

"Don't you just love our school uniform?"

I don't, I think. "I guess," I say.

"The smell of new school books, the fresh way our uniforms feel . . . I just love the start of a new school year."

At first I think Mirabel Plouffe is joking. But she looks smiley and far away, like she's daydreaming. I think she is actually excited about starting school tomorrow.

She looks at her fingernails. "My mother is going to paint my nails with clear polish. It is important to try to look your best at school. Especially on the first day. It is important to make a good impression, I think."

Mirabel Plouffe smiles at me like she is twenty feet tall. Like she is the queen of France and I am a toad. "I should go. But I will see you tomorrow, Winicker! I think you will be in my class." She wiggles her fingers at me and leaves.

I feel kind of choked, like I swallowed a big ice cube. I'm going to be in the same class as Mirabel Plouffe. I bury my face in my pillow again.

Grandma Balthazar is wrong. Tomorrow is going to be the worst day ever. Mirabel Plouffe's voice is in my head. *It is important to make a good impression, I think.*

I think about Grandma Balthazar's shiny new hair. I think about the bottle of silver hair dye in the bathroom cabinet. I think I have an idea.

Three

"Winicker Wallace, what is taking so long? You've been in that bathroom for half an hour!" Mom is pounding on the door. "There is one bathroom in this apartment, and other people need to use it!"

That is another thing I do not like about Paris. We have only one bathroom here. We had three bathrooms at home in Three Rivers. Nobody ever had to knock on the door and tell me to hurry up in Three Rivers. They could just go use one of the other bathrooms.

I squint at the hair dye instructions on the edge of the sink.

STEP FIVE: Rinse hair thoroughly.

I duck my head under the faucet and turn on the water.

"I need a minute. I'm supposed to 'rinse hair thoroughly.'"

Mom stops pounding on the bathroom door. "What did you say? You're rinsing your what?"

"My hair," I say. "I'm rinsing it 'thoroughly.'"

Mom is quiet for a second. Then she uses a very calm sounding voice. She uses this voice when she's mad. "Winicker, open this door immediately."

Uh-oh. I turn off the water. I look up at the mirror, and wow! My hair is silver! Well, sort of silvery-blue. And wet. It looks great! Just like Grandma Balthazar's hair.

My face doesn't look as great. It's streaked like a zebra. Some of the hair dye got on my shirt, too. I don't care. My shirt has a picture of the Arc de Triomphe on it. We visited the Arc de Triomphe last week. I didn't see what all the fuss was about. It looks like a big cement doorway that doesn't lead to anything.

I unlock the bathroom door. Mom's forehead looks crinkly and worried at first. But then her eyes get huge and her mouth opens. She looks very, very, very angry.

"Are you kidding me? You dyed your hair gray?! And your face is just—" Her voice gets louder and louder until she is shouting. "Winicker Wallace. You are ten years old, and it seems I can't even let you use the bathroom by yourself!"

I feel like I might cry.

Dad comes over and looks at me. "Yikes. That's pretty bad, Winicker. But I really need to use the bathroom. Could you two maybe talk about this in the kitchen or the living room?"

"No, Michael, we cannot," Mom says. Michael is what Mom calls Dad when she's mad at him. The rest of the time she calls him Dear. When Dad is mad at Mom, he calls her Alice. The rest of the time he calls her Sweetheart.

"We need to get as much of this stuff washed out of her hair as possible. Winicker's first day of school is tomorrow. She's going to walk into her new classroom looking like a senior citizen! Winicker, march." Mom points to the sink. She follows me over to it. "Head under the faucet, please."

I sigh. "That's what I was trying to do before you made me open the door. Rinse my hair thoroughly. And anyway, I dyed it silver."

Mom turns on the faucet. She takes the bottle of stinky lavender shampoo from the edge of the old bathtub. I duck my head over the sink again.

These are two more things I hate about Paris. The smell of the shampoo and the bathtub. In Three Rivers, we had a shower. Here, we only have a bath. I hate baths. A bath feels like I am being cooked in a big pot of soup. A bath feels like at any second a huge, hairy, people-eating monster is going to come out of the water and say "Bonjour, Winicker. I am going to eat you, starting with your tasty little toes." Just the idea makes me shiver.

"Please let me keep it. My hair looks great! I look like an individual." I love the word *individual*.

Grandma Balthazar taught it to me. It makes me feel special and unique, which is another word I love.

Mom pours a handful of shampoo into my hair. Then she scrunches my hair with her fingers, making everything foamy.

Dad is in the doorway making a sad face at the toilet. "I guess I can go use the Plouffes' bathroom," he says.

I can tell Mom is really upset because she is scrubbing my head and doing slow breathing. Her eyes are closed. She's probably counting to twenty in her head. One time, she told me she counts to twenty so her head won't explode. I'm pretty sure this is one of those times.

Mom turns off the water. She covers my head with a pearly peach towel and rubs my hair, hard. I want to say don't rub so hard! But I don't. I am worried her head is close to exploding, even after she counted to twenty.

She is rubbing my head so hard it kind of hurts. She is rubbing so hard I'm worried she's going to rub all of the silver out of my hair. *Please, please, please,* I think, *don't let the silver get rubbed out*!

Good news! My hair is still silver! As silver as a shiny new nickel! As silver as Mirabel Plouffe's weird chicken necklace! As silver as Grandma Balthazar's hair!

"Bad news," I say to Mom. "It's still silver." Mom sits down on the side of the bathtub. She looks tired.

Grandma Balthazar pokes her head in the bathroom. "Oh, Winicker," she says. "Well, you'll certainly look like an individual in room 3A."

Room 3A is my new classroom in my new international school. Mom told me the teacher will speak English and there will be kids from all different countries.

She told me my new school will be a lot like my old school. But I don't think that's true. My old school was called Three Rivers Elementary, and I could say it just fine. My new school is called La Petite École Internationale de Paris, and I can't say it at all.

I don't want to be in room 3A or in La Petite anything. I want to be in my third grade class with Roxanne. I'm glad Grandma Balthazar used the word *individual*, though.

"Oh, Winicker, you've even left gray streaks on my good towel." Mom looks at the towel like she is going to cry.

I look closely at the towel. "Silver," I say. "These are silver streaks."

"And you're just going to have to go to school in the morning with that hair. Honestly, Winicker." Mom sounds disappointed.

I look at the floor. For a second, I forget about my silver hair that makes me look like an individual. I didn't mean to disappoint Mom. I don't want to go to room 3A in the morning. I don't want to be in a class without Roxanne. And most of all, I do not want to sit anywhere near Mirabel Plouffe.

After I brush my teeth and get ready for bed, I sit at my desk. I start a postcard to Roxanne. When we moved here, Grandma Balthazar told me to write a postcard whenever I am missing someone. I am missing someone now. I reach for my 'Be Fri' necklace even though I know it isn't there.

Dear Roxanne,

I dyed my hair silver. I lost my 'Be Fri' necklace. I don't want to be in room 3A. It rains here a lot. I hope you are enjoying Three Rivers. I am not enjoying Paris. If this were a large box instead of a postcard, I would get inside and mail myself to you.

Love,
Winicker

Dad opens my door. "Can I tuck you in?"

I slip my postcard under my copy of *The Mouse and the Motorcycle*. It is my favorite book in the whole world. "Okay," I say.

I get in bed and let Dad pull the covers up to my chin. He kisses me on the forehead.

"You know, Paris is really a pretty cool place. The Plouffes next door have a bidet in their bathroom," he says.

"What's a bidet?" I ask.

"A water fountain for your bottom!" he says.

I laugh until tears squeeze out of my eyes. Dad smiles at me.

"I thought you'd think that was pretty funny. I sure did!"

"You didn't use the bidet, did you?" The idea of Dad using a bidet makes me cry-laugh all over again.

"No! Not to water my bottom. But I did turn it on. If our bathroom is ever too busy again, or out of order, you'll have to use theirs. Just to check it out. It's pretty wild."

I shake my head. "If our bathroom doesn't work, I'm going to go to one of the pay toilets on the sidewalk outside. I'm never using Mirabel Plouffe's bathroom. Not ever."

Dad shrugs. "Well, okay. But you're missing out on some very funny plumbing!"

Four

La Petite École Internationale de Paris doesn't look petite at all. It's a huge, gray building with too many windows. There are green vines up the side, and it's all wet. That's because it is raining this morning in Paris. It rains every morning in Paris.

There are all different kinds of weather in Three Rivers. Sometimes it rains there, and sometimes it doesn't. Sometimes it even snows.

I tug at my uniform collar. It's too chokey-feeling. I wish I could wear whatever I want. I always could at Three Rivers Elementary. At least I get to bring my favorite green backpack.

I am huddled with Grandma Balthazar under a big, gray umbrella. "Here's an idea," I say. "How about I get homeschooled? I read that some of the smartest people in the world were homeschooled, like Bill Gates and Marie Curie."

"You did not read that. And they were not homeschooled." Grandma Balthazar frowns. I feel like an inner tube that got poked with something sharp.

"Okay. Well, if I were homeschooled, I'd have a lot more time for things like cleaning my bedroom." I wiggle my eyebrows.

"Sorry, Winicker," Grandma Balthazar says. "You're going to school. Here's another idea. How about we go inside?"

She gives me a too-quick hug. "I know it's scary," she says. "But you're going to make some wonderful friends. And you'll learn brand-new, exciting stuff. This is an adventure! Just think of how many little girls in Three Rivers would love to go to school in Paris."

Well, what do they know, I think.

"It's going to be a wonderful year," Grandma Balthazar says.

Except it doesn't seem so wonderful when we walk up the big stone steps and I trip and fall and almost skin my knee. And it doesn't seem so wonderful when we can barely squeeze the two of us through the crowded hallway inside. And it doesn't seem so wonderful when everyone turns around and stares at my silver hair.

All the boys and girls are wearing the same uniform shirts as me. But exactly zero boys and girls have silver hair like me.

"Here we are," Grandma Balthazar says when we get to room 3A. She pushes the door open. There's a lady with frizzy brown hair and glasses with orange frames standing in front of the big desk in the front of the room. She runs over to us, dropping the papers she was holding.

"Bonjour! Hello! I am Mademoiselle Bennett!" Mademoiselle Bennett sounds out of breath.

"Please, come in, S'il vous plaît! How can I help you?"

"This is my granddaughter, Winicker Wallace. She'll be joining your class." Grandma Balthazar nudges me into the room. It feels a little like a push.

I like Mademoiselle Bennett already, but that's the only thing I like about room 3A. I don't like how the desks are all pushed together in groups of four. In my old classroom in Three Rivers, the desks were all singles. Nobody had to sit in groups.

I also don't like how Mirabel Plouffe is already here, sitting in a group of four. She probably got to school sixteen hours early. She gives me a big smile like we're best friends. We are definitely not best friends.

Mademoiselle Bennett claps her hands together. "Bonjour, Winicker! I am so happy you're joining us this year! Mirabel told me you two are already les copines, so I have seated you with her." She points at Mirabel Plouffe, whose smile gets even huger. I don't know what copines are, but I am sure we are not.

I don't want to sit anywhere near Mirabel Plouffe. But I don't know anyone else at this school. And I don't want to sit with a bunch of strangers.

Grandma Balthazar gives me a secret hand squeeze. "I hope you have the best day," she says.

I won't, I think. I definitely won't.

"I can't wait to hear all about it when I come to get you this afternoon."

Grandma Balthazar leaves, and I get a prickly feeling behind my eyeballs. Before any tears can sneak out, I pick my desk. It's diagonal to Mirabel Plouffe's desk. Diagonal means the farthest away from Mirabel Plouffe I can get, but still in the same group of desks.

Mirabel Plouffe is still smiling at me. "Ho! Winicker, your hair! You have dyed it gray!"

I want to make another pig nose at Mirabel Plouffe, but Grandma Balthazar said no more pig noses. "No, Mirabel Plouffe, I have dyed my hair silver, which is very different from gray."

I look at the clock. It is 8:35, and the school day begins at 8:40. A group of boys walks in. Their uniform ties are flung over one shoulder. They are smiling and laughing and talking in a language that isn't English or French. Two girls walk in behind them. They look like best friends. They remind me of me and Roxanne. My eyeballs feel prickly again. Then a girl with long red braids walks in. She marches right over to our desk group.

"I'm Maizy Durand," she says to me and Mirabel Plouffe. She drops her white backpack onto the floor and sits down right next to me. "Is your hair gray? It is! You have gray hair!"

I can already tell that Maizy Durand is going to be my enemy.

"It is silver," Mirabel Plouffe says. I wish she wouldn't say anything.

Maizy Durand gives me a mean sneer. "I think it's gray. You have gray hair, just like an old lady. You're like a little, tiny grandmother. La Petite Grand-mère. That's what I'm going to call you."

My face and neck feel really hot. I want to say a bad word. A really bad word. I want to say a word I heard Grandma Balthazar say one time when she thought no one was listening.

The door to room 3A bangs shut.

"Bonjour, class! I am Mademoiselle Bennett, and I'll be your teacher this year. I am from Minnesota. That's in Les États-Unis—the United States."

I don't know where Minnesota is. But I bet it is a lot closer to Three Rivers than Paris is.

"We're going to take exciting trips and learn some very exciting things. We will speak English in class, and we'll learn all kinds of things about France. I'll pass out a reading list in just a moment. First, I want each of you to introduce yourselves to the class. Let's start with Winicker Wallace. Please stand up, Winicker, and tell us about yourself!"

I do not want to stand up. I can tell everyone is looking at my hair. "I'm Winicker, and I—"

"What a name!" Mademoiselle claps her hands together and looks pleased. "Can you tell us what it means?"

"Well, I don't think it really means anything. I mean, it's not a word." I wish I were somewhere else. Especially back home in Massachusetts, where there is no Mirabel Plouffe. Or Maizy Durand. I clear my throat the way my dad does when he has something important to say. I try to feel brave.

"Winicker is the sound a horse makes," I say. "My dad read it in a book once. He liked the way it sounded."

I hear some of the kids whispering. Maizy Durand raises her hand. Nobody calls on her, but she talks anyway. "Did you see a ghost, Petite Grand-mère? Is that why your hair is so gray?" She bats her eyelashes and whinnies like a horse. "Neh-heh-heh-hey!"

Suddenly, before I can stop it, I feel Grandma Balthazar's very bad word bubble up my throat and right out of my mouth.

Grandma Balthazar meets me at the front of the school. The principal asked her to come early. I can always tell when she is mad at me. She walks faster, presses her lips together, and holds her head like she has a headache. That's what she is doing on our walk home from school.

"Wait a minute," I say. I'm almost running to keep up with her. "There was this really awful girl in my class. She kept saying awful things—"

"Honestly, Winicker. Not everything can be as awful as you say. Mirabel Plouffe is not awful. Your new school is not awful. And all of Paris cannot possibly be awful. You have to learn to take responsibility for your actions! You couldn't make it through a full day at your new school without an incident. Maybe if you'd try to have a better attitude, everything around you wouldn't seem quite so awful."

"I wasn't talking about—"

"I think we should probably just walk quietly until we get home. I am very disappointed. I think you have a lot of things to think about."

I feel like a heavy, black cloud is sitting on my shoulders. A cold raindrop rolls down the back of my collar. I wish Grandma Balthazar wouldn't walk so fast. The rain is rolling right off her umbrella and hitting me. I can't walk fast enough to stay underneath it.

I bet we look funny from behind with our matching silver hair. I bet we look like a couple of old friends who are having a fight. I do a very sad sigh. I feel like a couple of old friends who are having a fight. Grandma Balthazar is my only friend in Paris, and now I am very alone.

Five

When we get home, I go straight to my bedroom without anyone asking me. I don't want to be in the kitchen when Dad finds out I said a bad word in class and got sent home. I press my ear against the door. The sound is muffled, but I hear coffee cups clinking.

Then I hear Grandma Balthazar's high voice. " . . . no idea where she learned a word like . . . No, I . . . Disappointing."

I hear my dad's low voice, too. "I'll have a word . . . Just surprised, . . . never thought she'd have this trouble here."

I lie down with my face on my bed. My dad is going to come talk to me any minute now. His face is going to look disappointed and sad.

When my doorknob turns, I sit up and take a deep breath. I might be bad, but I can also be brave. This is what my dad calls facing the music.

"Winicker?" My dad looks exactly as disappointed and sad as I thought. "Your grandmother told me about what happened at school today." He sighs and sits down on my bed. "You aren't ecstatic to be here, huh?"

A big, fat tear that I was not expecting rolls out of my eye and down my cheek. "I don't know what ecstatic means, but I bet I'm not. It's nothing like Three Rivers here. It's nothing like Massachusetts. It just rains all the time, and I miss Roxanne. She makes the best fluffernutter sandwiches in the universe."

My dad nods his head. He looks like he knows how I feel.

More tears come out of me. "Grandma Balthazar says this is an adventure, but it doesn't feel like an adventure. It feels like I moved away from everything I like, and now we have to live in a place I don't like at all. I want to go home." The word *home* feels like a wad of pink bubble gum stuck in my throat.

My dad pulls me into a hug and kisses the top of my head. I feel very sad that I'm in Paris. But I'm very glad my dad is here with me.

"You know, this hasn't been an easy change for me either," my dad says.

I raise my eyebrows. I didn't expect him to say that. "It seems like an easy change for you. When Mom said 'they want me to run the Paris office,' you said, 'then let's move to Paris! I can write my book in Paris!' You're always in a good mood because they have bidets. And you never say anything bad about the rain or Mirabel Plouffe."

He smiles and scratches his chin. "Well, I guess I like to look on the bright side of things. I don't mind the rain or Mirabel Plouffe. And you really haven't lived until you've seen the Plouffes' bidet.

"But it made me sad to leave Three Rivers, because that was our home. We had you in Three Rivers. That's where you said your first words and took your first steps and lost your first tooth. I got a lot of my best writing done in Three Rivers, too. I haven't written more than a word since we've been here. And the word I wrote was *the*, which isn't even a very good word. But I know it'll get better. We just need to find all of the really great parts. Then the parts we don't like will seem very small."

"What are the really great parts?" I ask.

"Well, there are all of those great bakeries. Maybe we can go out for les macarons or des pains au chocolat when your mom gets home.

And there's the Eiffel Tower! We'll go this weekend. If it doesn't rain." Dad smiles. "And if it does rain, we can go the weekend after that. Best of all, Winicker, your family is here with you, and we love you very much."

I look out my window. The rain is making a hundred tiny rivers down the glass. More tears come out of me. I figure I must be all dried out like a desert on the inside. My dad hugs me tighter.

"Try to keep your chin up. It'll stop raining one of these days."

When my dad leaves, I add a PS to my postcard to Roxanne.

PS
I said a really, really bad word in class today. And I still miss you.

I stick the postcard back underneath *The Mouse and the Motorcycle*.

My mom is not in the mood for les macarons or des pains au chocolat when she gets home from work.

"I'm so sorry, guys," she says. She takes off her new pointy shoes with the red bottoms. "It was a long day at the office. I just want to take a long, quiet bath. Can I take a rain check?"

I want to yell "No! You cannot take a rain check!" But I feel lucky that no one has told my mom yet about the bad word incident. And I don't want to remind anyone by yelling.

My dad kisses my mom. "Of course. Grandma Balthazar, would you please make some of your famous macaroni and cheese? We'll just stay home and take it easy tonight."

"That sounds wonderful," my mom says.

"Of course," Grandma Balthazar says.

I'm glad I'm not going to get in trouble a third time for the same bad word. But I also wish I had pains au chocolat.

My mom locks herself in the bathroom. Grandma Balthazar starts boiling water and knocking pans and spoons around.

The doorbell rings.

My dad opens the door. I see a fancy red umbrella and shiny red boots. I can't see it, but I know the chicken necklace is out there, too.

"Winicker! You left so early today you were not there for our homework assignment. Quel dommage. But do not worry; I brought the assignment so you will not be behind tomorrow. If you are confused at all, I would be very glad to help you!"

My dad beams at Mirabel Plouffe.

Traitor, I think.

He takes Mirabel Plouffe's umbrella and sets it against the door.

"That's awfully nice of you, Mirabel! I'll get out of your way and let you two talk about homework." He winks at me.

Double traitor.

Mirabel Plouffe sits down next to me, even though I didn't ask her to. She hands me a folder with a picture of a puffy white cat on it. The cat reminds me of Grandma Balthazar's sweatshirt. The cat sweatshirt was ten thousand times better than the flowy blue shirt Grandma Balthazar is wearing now, with her flowy brown scarf wrapped around her neck too many times.

"The homework assignment is inside," Mirabel Plouffe says, as though I am very stupid.

I give her a mean look. "Why do you go to an international school when you're French? Why don't you just go to a French school?"

Mirabel Plouffe doesn't seem to notice my mean look. "Mes parents wanted me to learn about all kinds of cultures and languages by going to school with kids from all over the world. La Petite École is a wonderful school. I like to learn from the students as well as from the teachers."

Mirabel Plouffe probably wouldn't be so awful if she didn't speak like a human homework assignment all the time.

"Why don't you talk weird?" I ask.

"Winicker!" Grandma Balthazar shoots me an angry look from the stove.

"I mean why is your English so good?"

"I lived with my parents in England for two years," Mirabel Plouffe says. "When I was five and six."

"Oh." I thought Mirabel Plouffe had always lived in Paris. "Then you had to move across the world just like I did."

Mirabel Plouffe laughs into her hand. "Ho! No, Winicker, England and France are very close. England is just across the channel!"

Mirabel Plouffe also probably wouldn't be so awful if she didn't laugh at people and sound like a geography teacher all the time.

"Well," Mirabel Plouffe says, "if you are wondering about the assignment, we are to write one page about our favorite thing about Paris. I am very happy to help, if you need it! I know of many wonderful things in Paris that you could write about. If you have trouble thinking of something."

I would rather eat a giant slug than ask for Mirabel Plouffe's help.

"No, thanks. I got it. But I should probably get started soon, so . . ." I look at the door.

Mirabel Plouffe stands up. She looks uncomfortable. "Yes, I suppose you should! I finished mine before I watched the news this afternoon. I will see you tomorrow at school, Winicker. And, oh! I just wanted to tell you—I don't like Maizy either. I think she was just awful to you today. I don't blame you for saying that word in class."

Grandma Balthazar turns away from the macaroni to look at me again. She raises her silver eyebrows. As soon as Mirabel Plouffe leaves, Grandma Balthazar sits down next to me.

"I'm sorry I didn't listen, Winicker. On our walk home." I pat her on the shoulder.

Grandma Balthazar goes back to the macaroni and cheese. I hear her say, "This Maizy sounds like a bad banana."

I smile all the way, because Grandma Balthazar and I are friends again. But then I only smile half the way, because I really need to use the bathroom. I stand up and cross my legs and wiggle over to the bathroom door.

"I need to use the bathroom!" I yell to my mom, who is taking too long of a bath.

"Tough toodles!" my mom yells back. "I need this bath. I had a hard day at work. And don't think I haven't heard about your bad word! Go next door and use the Plouffes' bathroom."

Never! I think. I stomp into the kitchen.

"I need to use the bathroom bad," I tell Grandma Balthazar.

"Your father says the Plouffes have a bidet. That might be fun to see," Grandma Balthazar says.

I would rather pee in my pants than use the Plouffes' bathroom. Then I remember the pay toilet outside. I had to use a pay toilet when we went to the Arc de Triomphe. It was a toilet in a box, and you had to pay to use it. I'd rather pay a million dollars for a toilet in a box than use Mirabel Plouffe's bathroom.

I wiggle out our front door. I cross my legs and hop through the courtyard and up to the big, scary looking gate out front. I look down the street both ways, and there it is! The ugly gray pay toilet.

I dig change out of my pocket and *clink clank clink* it into the slot outside the pay toilet. The door opens. The inside of the pay toilet is dark and smelly. My eyes are burny from the smell. There is scary looking graffiti on the wall, but I don't care.

When I am finished using the bathroom, I rub hand sanitizer on my hands and try to open the door. It won't open. I push as hard as I can on the handle. Then I pull as hard as I can on the handle. The door won't budge!

"Help me! Can anyone hear me? I'm stuck in here! Help!"

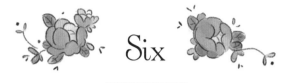

Six

"Please help me!" I bang on the door with both fists. I look for a help button, but all I see is more graffiti. And some chewed-up gum. And a wad of wet toilet paper stuck to the wall. "Help! I'm stuck in here! Can anyone hear me?"

I smoosh my ear against the door to try and hear someone walking by. I'll take a bath tonight. A double bath, maybe. I hear cars passing and the sound of a car horn. I do not hear Grandma Balthazar or Mom or Dad.

Grandma Balthazar and Mom and Dad don't even know where I am! My stomach feels like it is falling out of my body. I never told them I was going to use the pay toilet. They think I'm next door in Mirabel Plouffe's apartment!

They'll go looking for me though when I've been gone too long. And Mirabel Plouffe will turn off her dumb French news and tell them I never came to use the bathroom. Then they have to know I'm stuck in a pay toilet.

But . . . but maybe they'll think I stayed there and got Mirabel Plouffe to help with my homework. What if they think it's nice that we're finally getting along?

They will never come to look for me. I'm going to be stuck in this gross, dark box until I turn into a skeleton!

"SOMEONE PLEASE HELP ME! I'M STUCK IN THIS PAY TOILET!"

I put my hand over where my 'Be Fri' necklace used to be. I wish I had my necklace with me. I wish I had my best friend, Roxanne, with me. I wish I had anyone with me.

Mirabel Plouffe will watch the whole thing on her afternoon news show. She'll sip her tea and look very sad. She'll say, "How terrible. I wonder why she didn't just use our bathroom with its fancy French bidet?"

I wish I had used her bathroom. I wish I had seen the Eiffel Tower and all the other things in Paris that everyone thinks are so great. Instead, the last things I will see are graffiti I can't even read and a wad of toilet paper stuck to the wall of a pay toilet.

I am scared. I am scared-er than I have ever been in my entire life. I know I need to take a deep breath and calm down, but I can't. So I try to think about something else. Anything else. I've never been in a situation like this before. Except for maybe the other time I got trapped.

That was a whole two years ago, when I was six. Roxanne was six, too. Six is too young to know better. We were playing in Roxanne's backyard, and there was a shed next to Granny Bee's garden. It was a little purple-blue shed with a yellow roof. Granny Bee always told us not to go inside. There were gardening tools and spiders in there.

We always listened to Granny Bee. We never went in that shed.

But then, just one time, we didn't listen. We did go in that shed. Roxanne closed the door behind us so Granny Bee wouldn't look out the window and see us in the shed.

Granny Bee was right. There were gardening tools and spiders. Lots and lots of spiders.

There was a hole in the ceiling in one of the corners in the back. Under the hole, there was a bucket full of mucky rainwater.

"Ew," I said to Roxanne. "Look!"

Roxanne and I both leaned over the gross water bucket at the same time. Then we saw it! Floating around in the water was a dead snake. A real dead snake with scary dead snake eyes.

"AAAAAUGH!" we screamed. We ran to the shed door. Roxanne pulled on the rusty handle as hard as she could. But the door wouldn't open! I pulled on the handle, too, but we were stuck. We were stuck in the shed with the dead snake.

"AAAAAUGH!" we screamed again.

But then the door opened. Granny Bee was there! She'd heard us scream! She was mad we went in the shed. But we were happy to see her anyway. We never went in that shed again.

Also, it turned out there wasn't a dead snake in the water bucket. It was an old curled-up leaf.

But there's no Granny Bee to rescue me this time. There's no Roxanne in here with me, either. I am all alone, and I am going to be locked in here forever.

"LET ME OUT! LET ME OUT!"

"Winicker?" There's a voice outside the door of the pay toilet. "Are you inside?" The voice knows my name!

"Please, please help me! The door won't open, and I can't get out!"

I hear rustling, like the person on the other side of the door is digging for change. I hear *clink clink whirrrr*, and the door opens!

I have never been so glad to see Mirabel Plouffe in my whole life. I've never been so glad to see anyone in my whole life. Except maybe Granny Bee that time she opened the door to the shed. Mirabel Plouffe doesn't even look mad, the way Granny Bee did. She just looks confused.

I hug Mirabel Plouffe as tight as I can. She looks very surprised, but she hugs me back.

"How did this happen? Why were you in a pay toilet?" she asks. She looks like a surprised, curly-haired angel. An angel who goes around saving people trapped in pay toilets.

Before I can say anything, huge tears roll down my face. I shake my head. "It's a long story. Thank you for helping me."

Mirabel Plouffe smiles at me. "Of course! I am happy to help, Winicker!"

"What were you doing walking by, anyway?" I ask.

"Sometimes, when I have a writing assignment, I like to take a walk outside. The fresh air brings my imagination to life." Mirabel Plouffe breathes deeply. She is so weird.

We walk back to our building together. After we say goodbye, I walk into the kitchen.

The apartment smells like Grandma Balthazar's macaroni and cheese. My stomach does a happy wobble. Everyone is there at the table, talking and setting down dishes and jingling silverware.

I feel a little like I used to feel in my old Three Rivers kitchen. My heart does a happy wobble, too. I sit down.

"You guys will never believe what just happened," I say.

My dad smiles. "I told you the Plouffes' bidet was really something to see!"

"No," I try to explain, "that's—"

Grandma Balthazar squeezes my elbow. "Thank you for being so understanding about the bathroom, Winicker."

"Yes," my mom says. "I thought you might have been upset. But you headed right over to the Plouffes' and didn't make a fuss. I really needed that bath. Thank you, honey."

Understanding is not a word anyone has ever used about me before. I decide not to mention the pay toilet.

"No problem," I say. I dig the big spoon into the heaping, gooey bowl of macaroni and cheese.

Seven

The next morning, Mademoiselle Bennett smiles when I walk into the classroom.

"Winicker! I'm so glad to see you. I think we're going to have a much better day. I can just feel it." She pushes her glasses up higher on her nose. "Your friend Mirabel said she brought your homework over last night. So you should be all set. Are you all set? Do you have any questions?"

I shake my head. Mirabel Plouffe isn't exactly my friend, and I'm not exactly all set. But I don't have any questions, either. I drop into my desk, diagonal from Mirabel Plouffe.

"Bonjour, Winicker! What did you write about for your assignment? What is your favorite thing about Paris? A lot of students will say the Eiffel

Tower. Some will say Rose Bakery on Rue des Martyrs. They make the most delicious carrot cakes.

"For me, I said Shakespeare and Company is my favorite thing. My mother works there, so I go as much as I like. You may join me there at any time! Tonight, even. When I am there I can imagine all of the famous writers who used to go there, like Ernest Hemingway—"

"I wrote about my grandmother." I don't want to hear about her homework assignment. It's probably perfect. Everybody will love it, and someday they'll turn it into a movie.

"Your grandmother?" Mirabel Plouffe looks worried. "Oh no! But the assignment was to write about your favorite thing about Paris. For instance, I wrote about an actual place in Paris—"

"Yes, I know," I say. "But my favorite thing about Paris is that I'm with my grandmother. So that's what I wrote about."

I take my assignment out of the puffy white cat folder. I slide the folder to Mirabel Plouffe. I'm glad she saved me from the pay toilet, but she is still Mirabel Plouffe.

"Oh, you can keep the folder. But there are so many beautiful things to see in Paris. So many things to do!"

I frown and take back the folder. "We haven't done much yet. It rains all the time. Paris isn't so bad. I just like Three Rivers better."

Mirabel Plouffe's face looks very surprised, like she's never heard of someone not liking Paris.

More students take their seats. When Maizy Durand walks in, my stomach turns into a hard little ball. She marches over and sits down next to me.

"La Petite Grand-mère! You are back! I wondered if you would come to school today. Or perhaps if you would go to a retirement home, where the other grand-mères live."

My face feels very hot. I swallow hard to keep tears out of my eyes. The last thing I want is for awful Maizy Durand to see me cry.

"You stop it, Maizy." Mirabel Plouffe's face is even whiter, and her hands are clenched into small fists. "You leave Winicker alone."

"Are you her granddaughter? Is that why you're getting so upset, Mirabel? Do you visit your petite grand-mère in her retirement home every Sunday?"

Maizy Durand laughs a mean-sounding laugh. It reminds me of what a fox might sound like if foxes could laugh. I want to run away.

"All right, class!" Mademoiselle Bennett claps her hands together. She is still smiling, as though she did not hear Maizy Durand. "I am looking forward to your essays! I thought we might get to know each other a little better. Swap assignments with the student next to you. We will read each others' papers out loud."

I make a very unhappy face. Maizy Durand smiles a wicked smile at me and holds out her hand.

"Let's see your homework, Grand-mère. You did do your homework, didn't you?"

I feel like I am in a bad dream. I pinch my elbow just to check. It hurts a lot. I know I am not dreaming.

"Let's see it, Grand-mère."

I wish I had not written about Grandma Balthazar. Maizy Durand will never, ever forget the time La Petite Grand-mère wrote an essay about her grand-mère. Maybe my family will consider homeschooling now. I slide my paper to her. *Don't cry, don't cry, don't cry,* I tell myself.

Maizy Durand looks at my paper for a moment. Then she laughs again. "Oh, this is too good. Grand-mère, is this why you have such dull gray hair? You wanted to look just like your own grand-mère? Do you wear false teeth, too?"

"Maizy!" This time, Mademoiselle Bennett heard. "That is enough. Please put Winicker's paper down and walk to the principal's office. You can explain to the principal why you are there. I do not like unkindness in my classroom."

Maizy Durand's face turns a bright shade of purple. She looks at me and then at Mirabel Plouffe. She pushes back her chair. It makes a loud scraping sound on the floor. She slams the door behind her.

Mademoiselle Bennett smiles at me, but the rest of her face is sad. She squeezes my shoulder. "I was sometimes made fun of in school because of my glasses," she says. "And I happen to think your silver hair is lovely."

I feel better for a second, but then Mademoiselle Bennett walks away. Maizy Durand will come back, probably meaner than ever.

Mirabel Plouffe leans forward. "If you would like, I will read your essay to the class. You can read mine—"

"I don't need you to feel sorry for me, Mirabel Plouffe! Just leave me alone!" I want to run home. I want to run and run until I get to Three Rivers, Massachusetts.

Eight

At the end of the school day, Grandma Balthazar walks me home. We're both quiet again, but nobody is angry. I just don't feel like talking. I hate that I have to go to school with the meanest girl on the planet. There was nobody like Maizy Durand in Three Rivers.

Grandma Balthazar stops walking all of a sudden. I crash right into her. "Ow! Sorry, Grandma Balthazar. Why did you—"

"I think I know what the problem is, Winicker." Grandma Balthazar puts a hand on my shoulder.

"What problem? What do you mean?"

"You just haven't seen it yet. You haven't seen the best parts. Let's go." Grandma Balthazar turns around and walks quickly. I run after her.

"Where are we going?"

"To the Latin Quarter!"

I follow Grandma Balthazar down so many cobbled streets that my feet start to hurt. My backpack feels like it weighs a hundred pounds. "Are we almost there? My bag is so heavy!"

Grandma Balthazar throws her head back. "Hah! You think *your* bag is heavy? I've been carrying this around for a week!" She digs around inside her floppy gray purse and pulls out a chunky padlock. It is the size of her hand and as silver as both of our hair.

"Why have you been carrying that around?" I ask, rubbing my shoulder.

Grandma Balthazar winks. "You'll see. But first, you're about to have the best crepe of your life." She points down the street, and we keep walking.

We're in a place that seems totally different from where we live. There is nothing old or gray about this part of Paris. Here, the buildings look like they are dressed for a party.

I see lights on strings that hang above and all around them. This place is full of people speaking all different languages. They're eating all different foods from food stands.

The bright restaurant windows remind me of Christmas. Everything smells so good! I breathe deeply, the way Mirabel Plouffe did. "The fresh air brings my imagination to life," I whisper. This is probably what Mirabel Plouffe meant.

"What's that, dear?" Grandma Balthazar asks. "Are you hungry?"

My feet are so tired from walking on the bumpy cobblestones that I didn't even notice my grumbling stomach. "Yes!"

Grandma Balthazar brings me to a crepe stand that smells spicy and sweet at the same time. She orders two Nutella crepes. When the crepes appear at the window, Grandma Balthazar hands one to me. It is the best thing I have ever eaten! Warm and soft and filled with Nutella. It's even better than a fluffernutter sandwich.

Music pours into the streets from all of the restaurants. I squeeze Grandma Balthazar's arm.

"It's wonderful, isn't it?" Grandma Balthazar smiles down at me. "Welcome to Paris, my dear."

All of the women around us wear scarves around their necks like Grandma Balthazar. Some walk with their arms linked, like best friends. My heart hurts for Roxanne, but it only lasts a second. Grandma Balthazar looks at my face, and I can tell she knows. I'm mostly happy, but a tiny bit sad, too.

I put my hand up to my neck where my 'Be Fri' necklace used to be.

"Ah. We are still missing something."

I nod. "Roxanne."

Grandma Balthazar shakes her head. "Of course you miss Roxanne, and that won't change.

But I mean something around your neck. How about a scarf? Look around, my dear! You are missing a scarf."

Grandma Balthazar brings me to another stand. This one has lots of beautiful scarves on display. Pink ones, orange ones, yellow ones. Grandma Balthazar points to a beautiful bluey-green one. I nod my head. It's the most beautiful scarf I've ever seen.

Grandma Balthazar pays for the scarf and drapes it around my neck. She tucks the ends in, fluffs it up, and steps back. She smiles at me.

Grandma Balthazar is pretty good at finding the best parts of everything. I bet I'm standing right in the middle of the best part of Paris. I snuggle my nose down into my new scarf. I feel like I'm in Three Rivers at Christmas.

We walk down a long street and through a busy courtyard. Then we turn onto a wood plank walkway. I think it's a bridge, but I can't even see the water below. The railings are totally covered in padlocks. Just like the one Grandma Balthazar has in her purse.

"Are we going to put a lock on the bridge? There isn't any room!" I search the railings for a spot that isn't taken by one of the billions of padlocks that are already there.

Grandma Balthazar smiles and takes a marker out of her purse. "There." She points to an empty spot in the middle of a sea of locks. "Right there. Let's clip it on, and then we'll write our—"

Grandma Balthazar clicks the lock onto the bridge. Just then, her marker falls out of her hand and down into the river.

"Rats!" she shouts. Some of the people around us turn around to look at her. "Excuse me," she says to them. "Er, excusez-moi. Do you have a marker? A . . . pen? Un stylo?"

While Grandma Balthazar searches for a pen, I look at the railing behind me. The wind on the river is blowing my new scarf around my face. I breathe deeply. The Seine does not smell very fresh. I try to use my imagination to bring it to life, anyway. I bend closer to the railing to read the writing on some of the locks.

M.B. + N.B.
Mr. and Mrs. Embry forever
R.B.L. and Z.L. always, always, always.
Becky and Brandon!
J & L

I hug myself tightly and lean against the rail. Me and Grandma Balthazar are going to write our names on our lock, and it'll be here forever. Tourists and French people will read our names together for centuries.

The railing makes a sharp *squeeeak* all of a sudden. I jump backward. All of the padlocks on the panel I've been leaning on are shaking.

Squeeeeeeeeeak!

My stomach feels like it is going to fall out of my body. The chain-link railing is bending backward, toward the Seine. There are loud shrieks behind me. Grown-ups are running away from the railing. They're pushing each other, and they're pushing me!

I can't see Grandma Balthazar anymore. There are too many people between us. The whole side of the bridge looks like it's about to fall into the river! I feel like I'm in a very bad dream.

"Grandma Balthazar," I try to yell. "Grandma Balth—"

"Faites attention!" A man in a police uniform is running toward me from the other end of the bridge. "Arrêtez! Faites attention!"

I don't know what the police officer is shouting, but I know I am in very big trouble. I don't know where Grandma Balthazar is. I don't know what a French prison for ten-year-old girls might be like. I think *run*, and I run.

Nine

IT IS TOO EASY TO GET LOST

I run as fast as my aching feet take me. I run over the wooden planks of the bridge and through cobblestone streets. I run past tens and hundreds of unsmiling faces I don't recognize.

I run around street performers painted gold like statues and a man walking eight dogs on eight leashes. My heart beats hard in my chest when I almost bump into a mime in red suspenders and sad face paint. I don't know where I am.

I run and run, trying to find my way. Finally, my feet won't take me any farther. I sink down onto the sidewalk next to a rack of sunglasses outside a souvenir shop.

The sun is dropping behind the buildings. I try not to cry. Hot tears run down my face anyway.

I don't know where I am going. I'd run home, but I don't know where I live! The neighborhoods here are all numbered. Do we live in number eleven? Thirteen? I will never see anyone again. Not Grandma Balthazar, not my mom, not my dad. Not even Mirabel Plouffe.

Mirabel Plouffe. I take a big breath. I remember Mirabel Plouffe's favorite place in Paris. *"Shakespeare and Company is my favorite thing. My mother works there, so I go as much as I like. You may join me at any time! Tonight, even."* Tonight!

I feel a hand on my shoulder. A tiny old woman wearing a gold scarf and a pair of sunglasses looks down at me. "Ça va?" she says.

"I don't speak French!" I blubber.

"Ah." She nods her head. "Are you okay?"

"I'm lost! I don't know where I am. I don't even know my home address yet. But I might be able to meet someone. My friend." *My friend.*

I remember all of the bad things I've thought about Mirabel Plouffe. I remember the pig nose I made at Mirabel Plouffe through the window. I remember all the times I called her awful.

I hope the sunglasses woman can't tell how mean I am. I'm a terrible friend. I'm as mean and

nasty as Maizy Durand. I have got to be nicer to Mirabel Plouffe. If I ever see her again.

"Do you know where Shakespeare and Company is?"

The tiny woman claps her hands together and laughs. "Oui! Just there." I want to hug her. She points down the street. I squint to see a dark green shop with a yellow sign overhead. Shelves and carts and stacks of books sit outside.

"Thank you. Thank you so much! Um, merci!" I scramble up from the sidewalk and take off again. I try to ignore the pain in my feet. I run down the street until I'm panting in the doorway of Shakespeare and Company.

The front of the store smells like Dad's bookshelves! There's a cart of books next to the door. I see a book I know with a yellow spine sticking out just a little. *The Mouse and the Motorcycle.* I pull it out and squeeze it against my chest. I feel exactly like Ralph the mouse tonight. I feel like a very scared and small girl in Paris.

The bookstore is overflowing with books. The floor is a dark red color that makes me feel like the walls are shrinking. I head toward the back rooms, and I see even more stacks of books.

Between some of the shelves are red movie theater chairs. Sitting in one of the chairs is Mirabel Plouffe. She looks up at me over the book she's reading.

"Winicker? I am so glad you decided to come!"

For the thirty-thousandth time since my family moved to Paris, I burst into tears.

"I am the meanest and the most horrible person. I am really sorry about before," I sob into my hands on the red seat next to Mirabel Plouffe. "I just really miss Three Rivers. I didn't want to move, and then I had to, and you weren't Roxanne. You still aren't, but I'm okay with it." I sniff and wipe my nose on my sleeve.

Mirabel Plouffe pats my arm. "Of course you are homesick! That is perfectly normal. But I hope you will soon consider Paris your home. I am not Roxanne, I am sure. But I hope I can also be your friend."

I sniff again and try to smile at Mirabel Plouffe. "I hope so, too. About all of that."

Maybe, not this exact second, but someday, Paris will be my home. After all, Paris is where my parents live, and Grandma Balthazar, too.

Paris is where I go to school, even though awful Maizy Durand goes there too. And Paris is where Mirabel Plouffe lives. My friend Mirabel Plouffe. I actually like the way it sounds.

"I am very glad to see you. I have something I want to give you!" Mirabel Plouffe reaches into the pocket of her uniform sweater. She pulls out a tiny silver chicken on a silver chain. It's just like the one she is wearing around her neck.

"Oh!" I hold out my hand, and she drops the necklace into it. "Thank you! For my, um, chicken necklace!"

Mirabel Plouffe laughs. "This is not just a chicken, Winicker! It is a rooster. A rooster is a symbol of France. I wanted to give you the necklace to say welcome to this wonderful country. And to say I am glad to be your neighbor and your friend."

I throw my arms around her. "Thank you, Mirabel Plouffe," I say. "I'm glad, too."

I feel like crying again, but the happy kind of crying. I clasp the necklace around my neck and pat the chicken-rooster on top of my new bluey-green scarf. And I really am glad. I am also worried. Grandma Balthazar thinks I am lost, and I need to get back to the bridge.

"Can you help me find the lock bridge again?" I ask. "Grandma Balthazar is there. I kind of broke it. By accident. And then there were police, and I was scared, so I ran."

Mirabel Plouffe's eyes are very big. She has probably never had a friend who has run from the police before. I've never had a friend who has run from the police before, either, actually.

"The bridge is broken? And there were police? Let me just tell my mother where I am going." Mirabel Plouffe points to the doorway that leads to the front room of the store. "She is working tonight. She will let me help you find your grandmother. The bridge is not far at all."

Mirabel Plouffe and I leave Shakespeare and Company together. I take a deep breath of the air outside. It smells wet. It's going to rain again. But maybe the rain isn't so bad after all. It makes the streets and sidewalks sparkle.

Ten

PARIS ISN'T WHAT I EXPECTED

Grandma Balthazar's going to be proud of my new attitude about Paris and the rain and Mirabel Plouffe. Unless I'm in so much trouble for breaking the lock bridge and running away that Grandma Balthazar never wants to see me again.

We walk together through streets that seem even brighter and noisier now that the sun is setting. We pass the same mime I saw minutes earlier, but he looks less sad. We walk and walk, and I just know I'm going to be in big trouble.

When we finally get to the lock bridge, I want to run away all over again. Police officers in dark uniforms and construction workers in yellow hard hats shout things in French at tourists. They

wave everyone away from the part of the railing I broke.

I feel like a wet chunk of cotton is jammed in my throat. I try to swallow, but it doesn't help. At the other end of the bridge, I can see two police officers talking to a woman with sparkling silver hair. Grandma Balthazar!

"Over there!" I pull Mirabel Plouffe through the crowd of upset-looking tourists on the bridge. We pass the construction workers and officers and nearly crash into Grandma Balthazar.

"Winicker Wallace!" Grandma Balthazar is crying, and she smooshes my cheeks between her palms. "Do you have any idea how scared I was?"

I laugh even though I'm crying, too. "Do *you* have any idea how scared *I* was? I don't even speak French, for Pete's sake!"

Grandma Balthazar laughs. Mirabel Plouffe laughs. I laugh. The two police officers who were talking to Grandma Balthazar do not laugh.

"Est-ce Winicker?"

Grandma Balthazar nods. "Oui."

The officers look a little tired. They nod at Grandma Balthazar and then at me. One of them whispers something to the other. Then they join the other police by the broken railing.

"Grandma." I swallow. "I broke the bridge. I leaned on it, and the railing broke. It's my fault!" I point to where construction workers are attaching a thick piece of clear plastic over the hole in the droopy railing.

Grandma Balthazar squeezes my hand. "My dear, the locks are getting too heavy for the bridge. Those officers weren't upset with you for leaning on the railing. They were upset with me for bringing you here to add another lock! I wanted to find you and tell you it was alright. But I had no idea where to begin!"

Grandma Balthazar looks at Mirabel Plouffe. "Thank you, thank you, Mirabel, for bringing my granddaughter back to me. I don't know how you found her, but I am so glad you did."

Mirabel Plouffe beams at Grandma Balthazar as though she's just been given the French Person of the Year Award. Mirabel Plouffe sort of is the French Person of the Year. At least to me.

I link arms with her on one side and Grandma Balthazar on the other. We walk home together on the rain-sparkled streets.

That night, our kitchen is all warm and lit up. Dad brings a brown box over to the table, where I am sitting with Mom and Mirabel Plouffe and Grandma Balthazar. Mirabel Plouffe gets to stay with us for an hour until her mom gets home from work.

"This came for you today, Winicker," Dad says.

My name and my new address are on the box. They are written in my favorite handwriting in the whole entire world. The return address says:

ROXANNE RODRIGUEZ
150 Gilbertville Road
Three Rivers, MA 01080

"It's from Roxanne!" I say.

Dad is smiling at me. He already knows.

"Open it up," says Grandma Balthazar. "It must be something special!"

I rip off the clear packing tape and pull open the flaps of the box. There's some bubble wrap inside. I take it out and set it on the table to pop later. There is a postcard with a picture of the *Make Way for Ducklings* statues in Boston. I hug it to my chest for a minute. I miss the ducklings and Boston and Roxanne. Then I turn over the postcard and read what Roxanne wrote.

Dear Winicker,

I miss you a lot. I hope you are enjoying Paris. I also hope you are enjoying all of the fancy French food. But just in case you miss fluffernutter sandwiches, I am sending two out of three ingredients. (Granny Bee says you have bread in France. She wasn't sure about peanut butter or fluff. She says to say hi to Grandma Balthazar.)

Love,
ROXANNE

I pull out a jar of peanut butter and a jar of marshmallow creme. My eyes start to get teary, but in a happy way. I smile at my new friend Mirabel Plouffe.

"I'm going to teach you how to make a fluffernutter sandwich," I say.

I set up my fluffernutter work station at the counter. I spread a big glob of marshmallow creme over a slice of bread.

"What you want to do," I tell Mirabel Plouffe, "is make sure there's more fluff than peanut butter. You want fluff oozing out the sides of the sandwich. If you don't get it all over your hands, you didn't make it the right way."

I finish making the sandwich and hand Mirabel Plouffe the plate. She takes it to the table and sits down.

Grandma Balthazar has already finished eating her sandwich. Mom and Dad are almost done with theirs.

"These are better than I remember, Winicker!" Mom smiles at me.

"You're a rock star fluffernutter chef." Dad gives me a thumbs-up. "It seems like things in Paris aren't so bad after all."

"Things in Paris are definitely not so bad. I never found my 'Be Fri' necklace. But my new friend Mirabel Plouffe gave me this neat rooster one. And my hair is silver now, and we have fluffernutter sandwiches."

Dad squints. "Can somebody please tell me what a 'Be Fri' necklace is?"

Mirabel Plouffe takes a bite of her sandwich. "Ho! Winicker, this is delicious. I've never tasted anything like it! Would you write down the recipe for me?"

"Sure," I say. Leave it to Mirabel Plouffe to turn fluffernutter sandwiches into a homework assignment. But I don't actually mind. I don't actually mind at all.

R♡XANNE'S

Famous Fluffernutter Sandwich

INGREDIENTS

2 slices wheat bread

2.5 tablespoons marshmallow creme

2 tablespoons smooth peanut butter

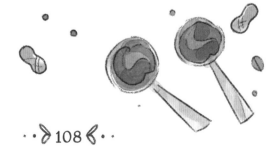

DIRECTIONS

Spread marshmallow creme on one side of one piece of bread. Spread peanut butter on one side of other piece of bread. Slap the pieces of bread together so the marshmallow creme and the peanut butter get all ooey and delicious and mixed up with each other.

Winicker Wallace's

Arrêtez: Stop

Bonjour: Good day

Ça va?: Are you okay?

Des Pains au chocolat: Puffy pastries with chocolate inside

Est-ce Winicker?: Is this Winicker?

Excusez-moi: Excuse me.

Faites attention!: Be careful!

Ho!: Oh!

La Petite École Internationale de Paris: The Little International School of Paris

La Petite Grand-mère: The Little Grandmother

Les copines: The friends

Les États-Unis: The United States

Les macarons: Very tasty cookies

Mademoiselle: Miss

Merci: Thank you

Mes parents: My parents

Métro: The subway system in Paris

Oui: Yes

Quel dommage: What a pity!

Rue des Martyrs: Martyrs Street

S'il vous plaît!: Please!

Un stylo: A pen

Meet the Author

Renee Beauregard Lute lives in the Pacific Northwest with one husband, two cats, and three amazing children. (Maddie, Simon, and Cecily, that's you!) There are many writers in the Pacific Northwest, and Renee is one of them. There may also be sasquatches in the Pacific Northwest, but Renee is not a sasquatch.

Like Winicker, Renee is from Western Massachusetts and loves macarons and sending postcards. Unlike Winicker, Renee has never lived in Paris, but she is very certain she would not hate it, even if Mirabel Plouffe lived next door.

Meet the Illustrator

Laura K. Horton is a freelance illustrator that has always had a passion for family, creativity, and imagination. She earned her BFA in illustration and animation from the Milwaukee Institute of Art and Design. When she's not working, she can be found drinking tea, reading, and game designing. Recently she has moved to Espoo, Finland, to obtain a master's degree in game design and development.